THOMAS C]

OF

CANTERBURY

BY

CHARLES WILLIAMS

British Library Cataloguing-in-Publication Data
A catalogue record for this book is available from
the British Library

CHARLES WILLIAMS

Charles Walter Stansby Williams was born in London in 1886. He dropped out of University College London in 1904, and was hired by Oxford University Press as a proof-reader, quickly rising to the position of editor. While there, arguably his greatest editorial achievement was the publication of the first major English-language edition of the works of the Danish philosopher Søren Kierkegaard.

Williams began writing in the twenties and went on to publish seven novels. Of these, the best-known are probably *War in Heaven* (1930), *Descent into Hell* (1937), and *All Hallows' Eve* (1945) – all fantasies set in the contemporary world. He also published a vast body of well-received scholarship, including a study of Dante entitled *The Figure of Beatrice* (1944) which remains a standard reference text for academics today, and a highly unconventional history of the church, *Descent of the Dove* (1939). Williams garnered a number of well-known admirers, including T. S. Eliot, W. H. Auden and C. S. Lewis. Towards the end of his life, he gave lectures at Oxford University on John Milton, and received an honorary MA degree. Williams died almost exactly at the close of World War II, aged 58.

THOMAS CRANMER
OF
CANTERBURY

A History of The Theatre

'The Theatre' is a collaborative form of fine art that uses live performers to present the experience of a real or imagined event. The performers may communicate this experience to the audience through combinations of gesture, speech, song, music, and dance, with elements of art, stagecraft and set design used to enhance the physicality, presence and immediacy of the experience. The specific place of the performance is also named by the word 'theatre' – derived from the Ancient Greek word *théatron*, meaning 'a place for viewing', itself from *theáomai*, meaning 'to see', 'watch' or 'observe'.

Modern Western theatre largely derives from ancient Greek drama, from which it borrows technical terminology, classification into genres, and many of its themes, stock characters, and plot elements. The city-state of Athens is where 'theatre' as we know it originated, as part of a broader culture of theatricality and performance in classical Greece that included festivals, religious rituals, politics, law, athletics, music, poetry, weddings, funerals, and symposia. Participation in the city-state's many festivals – and attendance at the City Dionysia as an audience member (or even as a participant in the theatrical productions) in particular, was an important part of citizenship.

The theatre of ancient Greece consisted of three types of drama: tragedy, comedy, and the satyr play (a form of tragicomedy, similar in spirit to the bawdy satire of burlesque). The origins of theatre in ancient Greece, according to Aristotle (384–322 BCE), the first theoretician of theatre, are to be found in the festivals that honoured Dionysus. These performances (the aforementioned City Dionysia) were held in semi-circular auditoria cut into hillsides, capable of seating 10,000–20,000 people. The stage consisted of a dancing floor (orchestra), dressing room and scene-building area (skene). Since the words were the most important part, good acoustics and clear delivery were paramount. The actors (always men) wore masks appropriate to the characters they represented, and each might play several parts.

Athenian tragedy (the oldest surviving form of tragedy) emerged sometime during the sixth century BCE, and flowered during the fifth century BCE – from the end of which it began to spread throughout the Greek world – and continued in popularity until the beginning of the Hellenistic period. Aeschylus, Sophocles, and Euripides were masters of the genre. The other side of the coin – Athenian comedy, is conventionally divided into three periods; 'Old Comedy', 'Middle Comedy', and 'New Comedy'. Old Comedy survives today largely in the form of the eleven surviving plays of Aristophanes, while Middle Comedy is largely lost (preserved only in a few relatively short fragments in authors such as Athenaeus of Naucratis). New Comedy is known primarily from the substantial papyrus fragments of Menander.

Western theatre developed and expanded considerably under the Romans. The theatre of ancient Rome was a thriving and diverse art form, ranging from festival performances of street theatre, nude dancing, and acrobatics, to the staging of Plautus's broadly appealing situation comedies, to the high-style, verbally elaborate tragedies of Seneca. Although Rome had a native tradition of performance, the Hellenization of Roman culture in the third century BCE had a profound and energizing effect on Roman theatre and encouraged the development of Latin literature of the highest quality for the stage. This tradition fed into the modern theatre we know today, and during the renaissance, theatre generally moved away from the poetic drama of the Greeks, and towards a more naturalistic prose style of dialogue. By the nineteenth century and the Industrial Revolution, this trend continued to progress.

In England, theatre was immensely popular, but took a big pause during 1642 and 1660 because of Cromwell's Interregnum. Prior to this, 'English renaissance theatre' was witnessed, with celebrated playwrights such as William Shakespeare, Christopher Marlowe and Ben Jonson. Under Queen Elizabeth, drama was a unified expression as far as social class was concerned, and the Court watched the same plays the commoners saw in the public playhouses. With the development of the private theatres, drama became more oriented towards the tastes and values of an upper-class audience however. By the later part of the reign of Charles I, few new plays were being written for the public theatres, which sustained themselves on the accumulated works of the previous decades. Theatre was now seen as something sinful and the Puritans tried very hard to drive it out of their society. Due to this stagnant period, once Charles II came back to the throne in 1660, theatre (among other arts) exploded with influences from France, and the wider continent.

The eighteenth century saw the widespread introduction of women to the stage – a development previously unthinkable. These women were looked at as celebrities (also a newer concept, thanks to ideas on individualism that were beginning to be born in Renaissance Humanism) but on the other hand, it was still very new and revolutionary. Comedies were full of the young and very much in vogue, with the storyline following their love lives: commonly a young roguish hero professing his love to the chaste and free minded heroine near the end of the play, much like Sheridan's *The School for Scandal*. Many of the comedies were fashioned after the French tradition, mainly Molière (the great comedic playwright), again harking back to the French influence of the King and his court after their exile.

After this point, there was an explosion of theatrical styles. Throughout the nineteenth century, the popular theatrical forms of Romanticism, melodrama, Victorian burlesque and the well-made plays of Scribe and Sardou gave way to the problem plays of Naturalism and Realism; the farces of Feydeau; Wagner's operatic *Gesamtkunstwerk*; musical theatre (including Gilbert and Sullivan's operas); F. C. Burnand's, W. S. Gilbert's and Wilde's drawing-room comedies; Symbolism; proto-Expressionism in the late works of August Strindberg and Henrik Ibsen; and Edwardian musical comedy. The list continues! These trends continued through the twentieth century in the realism of Stanislavski and Lee Strasberg, the political theatre of Erwin Piscator and Bertolt Brecht, the so-called Theatre of the Absurd of Samuel Beckett and Eugène Ionesco, and the rise of American and British musicals.

Theatre itself has an incredibly long history, and despite the massive proliferation of theatrical styles and mediums – it essentially owes its existence to the ancient Greeks and the Romans. The three main genres; tragedy, comedy and satyre, continue to influence plot themes, directing, writing and acting, with frequent and fascinating interrelations and overlaps. As a genre, it remains as popular today as it has ever been, and continues as a massive influence on popular culture more broadly. It is hoped that the current reader enjoys this book on the subject.

My thanks are due to the Friends of Canterbury Cathedral who, through Miss Babington, offered me the opportunity of writing this play; then to the Bishop of Chichester, Mr. Montgomery Belgion, Mr. E. Martin Browne, Mr. Hubert Foss, and Mr. Laurence Irving, who have all shown me kindness a proper acknowledgement of which would need the skill of Cranmer's own prose.

C. W.

PERSONS

THOMAS CRANMER

HENRY VIII

MARY

ANNE BOLEYN

FIRST LORD

SECOND LORD

A BISHOP

A PRIEST

A PREACHER

THE COMMONS

TWO EXECUTIONERS

ATTENDANTS

THE SINGERS

FIGURA RERUM: A SKELETON

PART ONE

The SINGERS *enter and take their places.*

THE SINGERS. God, the protector of all that trust in thee, without whom nothing is strong, nothing is holy; Increase and multiply upon us thy mercy; that, thou being our ruler and guide, we may so pass through things temporal, that we finally lose not the things eternal: Grant this, O heavenly Father, for Jesus Christ's sake our Lord.

Amen.

[*The* PRIEST *and the* PREACHER *run on.* CAM-
BRIDGE

THE PRIEST. The Lord remember you!   1528

THE PREACHER.   The Lord remember you!

THE PRIEST. Because you have forsaken him alone,
the Lord shall smite you with scabs and emerods.

THE PREACHER. Because you have followed lying gods,
the Lord shall set over you gods of stone.

THE PRIEST. Atheist!

THE PREACHER.   Idolater!

THE PRIEST.   Beast!

THE PREACHER.   Devil!

Will you silence God's Word?

THE PRIEST. Will you touch God's altar?

You shall come to the fire with your hands in a halter:

THE PREACHER. And the Lord shall fling you to your own
evil.

[*They fall apart.* CRANMER *enters.*

1

CRANMER. From riding to reading sweetly the days go.
I praise God for his space of Cambridge air,
where steeds and studies abound, that my thighs,
body and mind, have exercise,
each o'erstriding his kind, in beast or word.
Steed and speech go reined and spurred. I learned
easier the riding than the reading; I took
tenderness rather than tyranny and made my gain:
but now in strengthened brain I master the twain.
Coming in from the gallop, I vault on language, halt
often but speed sometimes, and always heed
the blesséd beauty of the shaped syllables. I would let go
a heresy or so for love of a lordly style
with charging challenge, or one that softens a mile
to a furlong with dulcet harmony, enlarging
the heart with delicate diction. Come,
to-day's journey waits: open gates! Blessed Lord,
thou hast given me horses, books, Cambridge, and peace:
foolish the man, having these, who seeks increase.
THE PRIEST. Roar, Antichrist: reach a ravin of hands.
THE PREACHER. Rage, Antichrist: wrap the Lord in bands.
THE PRIEST. Here is Christ, in a secret sacrificed.
THE PREACHER. Here, the Word witnessing, here is Christ.
CRANMER. Yet ah for the wars! here too must we wring
soul's duty out of that beauty: *verba verbera*—
even sluggards as I; I have sought,
read, thought, these three years, thought, read.
Appears now what was said:

THOMAS CRANMER OF CANTERBURY

In the beginning was the Word.
The Word was with God and the Word was God—
his disciples heard; his feet ran to the rood;
he gave himself to the souls of all holy living—
This is my body; take, eat:
Drink this; this is my blood:
feed on this in your heart by faith with thanksgiving.

> [*The* BISHOP *enters, vested, with acolytes and incense,*
> *and goes round the stage.*]

But now is man's new fall: now the fresh creature,
his second nature, nurtured by grace from the old,
lusts to withdraw itself and withhold
from the lawful food of God's favour; it lies
on the sea-broad floor of the Church, and its eyes
shut themselves on the steep sacramental way,
for it beats its heart in a half-sleep,
blindly covered by that panoply's art it was bid
rid itself of; multiple show and song
throng in its dreams the bare step of the Lord
and are adored in comfortable fearful respect.
It rises to genuflect where ceremony and rite
compose a moon-bright image. O in Paradise—
cries the tale—when Adam saw
himself in Euphrates, false awe and false delight
threw him to a plight of self-circling adoration,
where salvation's way was lost, which Christ restored
in means of communion; now are means of communion
   adored

THOMAS CRANMER OF CANTERBURY
yet dyked from approach; untrod, unexplored,
is the road; instead of God are God's marvels displayed,
rivals to Christ are Christ's bounties made,
and dumb are our people: negligent they lie and numb.

> [*The* PRIEST *and the* PREACHER *take place at the back
> of the stage.*]

Our Father, in whom is heaven, thy kingdom come.

> [*The* SKELETON *enters, carrying the crozier. He
> crosses the stage to the steps.*]

THE SINGERS. Blessed is he that cometh in the name of the
　　Lord; Hosanna in the highest.
THE SKELETON. Fast runs the mind,
　　and the soul a pace behind:
　　without haste or sloth
　　come I between both.

　　There blows a darkening wind
　　over soul and mind:
　　faith can hear, truth can see
　　the jangling bones that make up me:

　　till on the hangman's day,
　　and along the hangman's way,
　　we all three run level,
　　mind, soul, and God or the Devil.
CRANMER. O that the King, O that God's glory's gust
　　from heaven would drive the dust of the land, smite
　　his people with might of doctrine, embodied raise
　　their subservient matter, set with his fire ablaze

their heavy somnolence of heavenly desire, his word
bid what God said be heard, what God bade be done!
that the King's law might run savingly through the land:
so might I, if God please, outcast from my brethren stand.

THE SKELETON. We of heaven are compassionate-kind;
we give men all their mind;
asking, at once, before they seek, they find.

We are efficacious and full of care;
why do the poor wretches shriek in despair?
They run; after each, entreating him, runs his prayer.

Populous with prayers is the plain of Paradise,
skirring after the men who prayed, whose cries
beseech heaven to refrain; heaven hears not twice.

THE SINGERS. O how amiable are thy dwellings, thou Lord
of hosts!

THE SKELETON. We see our servant Thomas; we see
how pure his desire—Amen; let his desire be.

> [*Trumpet. The* KING, ANNE BOLEYN, *the* LORDS, *and* 1529
> *the* COMMONS *enter. The* KING *takes his throne; the*
> LORDS *retire to the back of the stage; the* COMMONS
> *go to their own place.*]

THE SINGERS. Give the King thy judgments, O God; and
thy righteousness unto the King's son.

Then shall he judge thy people according unto right;
and defend the poor.

The mountains shall also bring peace; and the little hills
righteousness unto the people.

He shall keep the simple folk by their right; defend the children of the poor, and punish the wrong doer.

They shall fear thee, as long as the sun and moon endureth: from one generation to another.

He shall come down like the rain into a fleece of wool: even as the drops that water the earth.

In his time shall the righteous flourish; yea, and abundance of peace, so long as the moon endureth.

His dominion shall be also from the one sea to the other: and from the flood unto the world's end.

THE KING. Hither, Thomas.

> [*The* SKELETON *goes to* CRANMER, *touches him, and brings him to the* KING. *He kneels. The* SKELETON *stands between and behind them.*]

Thomas, I am married to
a Death.
The lives I sow are slain in the woman's blood.
Corpse-conceived is the heir of my kingdom and power.
My soul is the power of God over this land:
my soul pines; the land dies; counsel the King.

CRANMER. Omnipotent sir—

THE KING.   The Pope's throat is thick.
His cold was caught in the Alps; Christ's image
is worked by German cords to mechanical glory.
My mind misgave me; God confirms me; my children
die, for my seed is drowned in my brother's blood.

CRANMER. Sir, the doctors deny the dispensation:

Oxford, Cambridge, Paris, Orleans, Toulouse,
Padua, Bologna; the Pope at first refused it.

ANNE. Henry, Henry, Henry, make me a wife.

THE KING. I saw a face that set me free from fate,
and made me pure to free the fate of the land,
by love, by a daughter of England, by Anne Boleyn.
I must have Anne, Anne with an heir by Anne,
legally mine, canonically mine.
There are no ghosts of children in her chamber
frightening me with white bones when I go in;
the mitred skeleton of Rome at the door
points in with the hand and trips me with the foot,
spectrally mouthing secret words; on the bed
beyond him is Anne, live children playing by her.
I labour, I labour, with the need of the deed.
Can any man anywhere unmake the King?

CRANMER. The imperial crown and jurisdiction temporal
of this whole realm are drawn direct from God:
within Christ's law there is none above the King.

THE KING. There must be found a means to make the
marriage.
The Pope nods from a corner. Archbishop Warham
is dead, as dead as Catherine's sons; he swore
that I was head of this Church, saving Christ's law.
Am I not head?

CRANMER.   Absolute head.

THE KING.   The oaths
to Rome?

CRANMER. Great sir, no oath has any force,
nor can be taken, nor should be understood,
to spoil a tittle of a subject's duty
unto the absolute Crown and Seat of England.

ANNE. Henry, Henry, Henry, make me a queen.

THE KING. There must be an archbishop to beget me an heir
legitimately and canonically.

THE
ARCH-
BISHOPRIC
1533 I am the head. Be Canterbury, Thomas.
The Pope nods to me; he will send the pall.

CRANMER. Sir!

THE KING. Be Canterbury: help me beget an heir.
I am turmoiled each way with desire and hope.
Be swift; determine the cause; pronounce this month
the dispensation invalid, the marriage null.
Terrible to the land is the trouble of the King.

CRANMER [*standing up*]. I am no man for this; I am pur-
blind,
weak, for my courage was shouted out of me
by schoolmasters and other certain men.
My thought is slow, uncertain of itself,
willing to serve God and its friends and peace—

THE KING. The will of the King is as the will of God.

THE SKELETON [*giving the crozier to the* KING, *who hands it to*
CRANMER]. Besides, even your thought must consider
your world,
and a little hurry to be of use to your world.
Even a shy man must make up his mind.

Has not much adoration quenched communion?
Must not Christ intend to restore communion?
Now is your chance, Thomas, to serve Christ!
CRANMER. I am God's servant and the King's.
THE KING.   Go then,
and make me, as I am, irretrievably Anne's.

[CRANMER *is vested.*

THE SINGERS [*during the vesting*]. O how amiable are thy
dwellings: thou Lord of hosts!

My soul hath a desire and longing to enter into the
courts of the Lord: my heart and my flesh rejoice in the
living God.

Yea, the sparrow hath found her an house, and the
swallow a nest where she may lay her young: even thy
altars, O Lord of hosts, my King and my God.

Blessed are they that dwell in thy house: they will be
always praising thee.

Blessed is that man whose strength is in thee: in whose
heart are thy ways.

Which going through the vale of misery use it for a
well: and the pools are filled with water.

They will go from strength to strength: and unto the
God of gods appeareth every one of them in Sion.

[CRANMER *goes to* ANNE.

ANNE. Make me irretrievably, irretrievably the King's.
CRANMER. The King is masked with his majesty; all we are
tasked

to be shaped at his will, infiltrated with his colour,
whether for dolour or peace. You must have no sense,
madam, but of this spiritual obedience
to make you in mind and feature the King's creature,
as the King is God's; be you the image of God's image.

ANNE. I have seen an image of myself:
a golden-shoed, crowned, and red-mouthed image,
which the King holds in his hands over his lands.
Some kiss its feet, some its mouth.

CRANMER. Feet to run, mouth to bless the King;
he is the stress of our hearts to heaven. Come,
madam, I will bring you to him; you are his bride.

ANNE. Henry, I am the queen; I will be your wife.
Henry, Henry, Henry, kill my enemies.

THE KING. Why, sweetheart, this is a holiday in heaven:
God is placable to the land, as I to you.
Look now, the land has peace
for I am quiet, and you are placable to me:
this will be sealed and revealed in the coming of an heir.
You have done well, Archbishop; get to your tasks.
Make a single kingdom for the prince of the kingdom.

[CRANMER *goes out.* ANNE *sits at the* KING'S *feet.*

THE SKELETON. Anne had a vision of an image in the King's
hand.
The land also has visions. Speak; I permit you.

VOICES FROM THE COMMONS. Adoration!
Communion!

THOMAS CRANMER OF CANTERBURY

Adoration!

Communion!

Up with the clergy!

Down with the clergy!

Texts and the Councils!

Texts and the Fathers!

Jesus, have mercy!

Antichrist!

Antichrist!

They lie in hell; death gnaws upon them!
Shibboleth!

Shibboleth!

Abracadabra!

THE SKELETON. Hark, the images go abroad!
Once in a way, once in an age,
when men's spirits rage, I set the images free,
all idols of hall, chapel, and marketplace,
spectral images, lacking love's grace, of me.
Their foreheads' phosphorescence shines;
they make signs; then one man walks, one talks,
under those moons, and in action and speech
each grows a wicked automaton to each,
a diseased bone, to be flung to Gehenna;
yet I only am the pit where Gehenna is sprung.
Brother reason and sister experience spew at each other,
sister dogma and brother denial run askew.
Then all but the hearts of the blessed ones dance
askance from love of Christ to love of corruption,

B

crying maniacally *Abracadabra,*
abracadabra, abracadabra.
But through their delirium I walk like a blind
beggar, pleading for a man to be kind;
the Son of Man walks backward on their way,
crying *Do you hear me? where is the way?*
O my people, where is the way?

> [*He goes round the stage, as if blind and begging,*
> *saying.*]

O my people, where is the way?
Do you hear me, zealots? where is the way?
THE PRIEST. Accipe; this is the way.
THE PREACHER.   Audi; this is the way.
THE COMMONS. This, we heard, was the way.
THE LORDS.   This, we feel, is the way.
THE KING. This that I bid is the way.
THE COMMONS.   This—is not this—
     the way?
THE SKELETON [*to the audience*]. Yet, O my people—can you
     believe it?
   blessed and chosen are they who receive it—
   there is a way; I am the way,
   I the division, the derision, where
   the bones dance in the darkening air,
   I at the cross-ways the voice of the one way,
   crying from the tomb of the earth where I died
   the word of the only right Suicide,

the only word no words can quell,
the way to heaven and the way to hell.

[*He goes round the stage, singing.*

I am the way, the way to heaven;
who will show a poor blind beggar the way to heaven?
I am the way, the way to hell,
who will teach a poor blind beggar the way to hell?

[*The figures break into movement.*

I am the way, the way to salvation,
who will desire the way of salvation?

[*He runs round the stage; they all follow him. Presently he stops, and sits on the steps.*]

I am the jawbone of the ass
on which, it is said, it came to pass,
Christ rode into Zion; Zion gleams askance.
Let us hear what my people make of this dance;
especially what my Thomas makes of the dance.

[*The figures are still—the* KING *stands up.*

But what, in the interval, is this? the King had his desire: 1534–6
does he run so soon after heaven to be rid of his desire?

[CRANMER *re-enters.* ANNE *falls at the* KING'S *feet.*

THE KING. Thomas, Thomas, Anne is not what I thought.
THE SKELETON [*speaking over the audience*]. A remark few of
   you die without making,
[*Over his shoulder to* CRANMER]
   nor shall you die without making,
   but, for your comfort, of a lordlier substantive.

[*To the audience*]

That is all I can ever promise any of you,
but much peace depends on the kind of substantive.

THE KING. Go; question; report; find out all.

THE SKELETON [*rising*]. Come, Thomas; we will go to Anne
who also had her desire and now cries to heaven.
Good or bad, you all come to it in the end.

[*He and* CRANMER *go to* ANNE *and raise her.*

THE SKELETON. Is your image broken, Anne?

ANNE.   I wanted so little:
only the Crown because it lay in my way,
and a few small pleasures—variations from Henry.

THE SKELETON. If you had asked for the greatest conceivable
things,
as Thomas does unintentionally, they would cost no more.
The price of heaven or hell or the world is similar—
always a broken heart, sometimes a broken neck.

ANNE. My neck is small: will the King have it cut?
He loved me—once.

CRANMER.   Madam, repent, confess,
entreat; the King is gracious.

THE SKELETON.   Heaven is gracious,
but few can draw safe deductions on its method.
Turn your eyes; look at me.

ANNE.   Archbishop, I have a secret—
hark!—that may save me.

[*She whispers.* CRANMER *goes to the* KING.

THE KING. She shall die.

CRANMER. Sir—

THE KING. She shall die.

CRANMER. If indeed—I can hardly believe—

THE KING. I say, she shall die.
She has taken my image of her love and broken: she dies.

CRANMER. Sir, all men have sinned: your highness has sinned.

THE KING. You are full of a silly innocence, Archbishop.
I say, she dies.

THE SKELETON. Turn your eyes; look at me. I
am the broken image, the bones of the image, the image
taken away from me and I from the image.

ANNE. What does King Henry say?

CRANMER. Alas, madam,
ira regis mors—the wrath of the King is death.

> [*The* SKELETON *covers* ANNE *with his cloak; they go
> out,* CRANMER *following. The* KING *seats himself.
> The* LORDS *kneel at the sides of the Throne.*]

THE FIRST LORD. Most mighty sir, regard the spirituality.

THE SECOND LORD. Regard, most mighty sir, the sins of the
monks.

THE FIRST LORD. Reckon meadow and pasture—one-fourth
the realm.

THE SECOND LORD. Compute paten and pyx, chalice and
cope.

THE FIRST LORD. Sir, the need of the government!

THE SECOND LORD. The simplicity of Christ!

THE FIRST LORD. Sir, for the Crown's need's sake—

THE SECOND LORD.   for Christ's gospel's sake—

BOTH THE LORDS. it were right the Lord of England received
    the richness.

THE FIRST LORD. Inflaming their bestial appetite with
    spiritual lust,

THE SECOND LORD. fornications with pomp, adulteries with
    power,

THE FIRST LORD. betraying the poor vows they swore to keep,

THE SECOND LORD. abusing their virginal conformity with
    Christ's mind,

THE FIRST LORD. basely and turbulently collecting earth's
    treasure,

THE SECOND LORD. besides fornications and adulteries of the
    common sort,

THE FIRST LORD. such as we dare not name for mere modesty,

THE SECOND LORD. whereby their hearts' brothels enrich
    damnation,

BOTH THE LORDS. it were well the Lords of England had
    their wealth.

THE FIRST LORD. Sir, behold a formula—a device fitted,

THE SECOND LORD. a confession due to the King of criminal
    follies;

THE FIRST LORD. those that will sign—simple men misled,

THE SECOND LORD. Sir, dissolve them graciously; take the
    land.

THE FIRST LORD. Those that stand obstinately in sin, contending

THE SECOND LORD. that they never did what we have written they do—

THE FIRST LORD. or that some do; if they deny that all do,

THE SECOND LORD. Sir, dissolve them mightily; seize the gold.

BOTH THE LORDS. It were good the gentry of England had their goods.

[CRANMER *returns; and the* SKELETON.

THE KING. This many ancient Catholic kings have done,
even my predecessor, Henry the Fifth.
If the monks and the guilds are as sinful as they say
it were well the King of England had the land.

THE FIRST LORD. It were better, sir, that it were given to us.

THE SECOND LORD. Then we shall know you right defender of the faith,

THE FIRST LORD. And that Anne was either legitimate or not—

THE SECOND LORD. as your Highness pleases; she having died somehow,

THE FIRST LORD. and your Highness having a quite undoubted heir,

THE SECOND LORD. as long as the lands are quite undoubtedly ours.

THE KING. Thomas, Thomas!

[CRANMER *comes to the* KING.

                                    Thomas, am I afraid?
Boars and bulls root at me and butt me.
Anne confessed; you went to Anne; she confessed.
CRANMER. Sir, she confessed.
THE KING.   When you went friendly to her?
CRANMER. God help me, sir, I cannot bully; I went
    friendly. I have searched my heart often to know
    if I went too friendly; she and the Nun of Kent,
    poor creatures, shut in prison, and I went,
    speaking them softly; did I speak too soft?
    I cannot shout, but what they said I told.
    If I deceived—did I deceive? I desired
    justice to the prisoners, justice to the King.
THE SKELETON. You shall have it, Thomas, justice for your-
    self;
    trap for trap, honour for honour, prison for prison;
    love, in the end, for love. We will play fair.
THE KING. Stand by me, Thomas. I am the King.
    I need no help; only stand somewhere near me.
    There is blood running over gold in all men's eyes,
    yours are clear, but worn with looking on books.
THE SKELETON. With the grand hydroptic desire of humane
    learning,
    as says a priest of Paul's, bended and boned
    to my frame, a master of this same wisdom,
    but of deaths also and other lores disowned;
    and a greater than he, another John than Donne,
    felt Christ's feet spurning such learning:

But you, poor man, think it good and better than Anne!

THE KING. You have been a picker of quarrels with me, my
    lord,

over my book: I told the Bishop of Winchester

you were too old a truant for him and me.

CRANMER. Archbishop and the King's servant though I be,

I am everywhere out of place but among books

where past voices make canticles of peace.

THE SKELETON. Anne had an image of the Crown—she is
    dead;

it is sped, the image that the King had of Anne.

Are words wiser than women or worship? safer,

securer, purer? will you hierarchize the glancings

of everywhere the translucent golden-tinctured wafer

on men's eyes, the webbed light of the glory

wherein is the angle of creation; along those lines,

up and down my sides, communion and adoration

flow and ebb and flow. Beckon your image,

call and repel it, serve and slay it.

Till the day when I sound its knell and yours as well,

have, have, have your will,

for what it is worth, precisely what it is worth;

have, have, have your prayer.

CRANMER. Pray we, all humble readers, for the grace of God: THE

ENGLISH

Blessed Lord, which hast caused all holy Scriptures to be BIBLE

written for our learning 1537

THE SINGERS. grant that we may in such wise hear them,

read, mark, learn, and inwardly digest them, that, by

patience, and comfort of thy holy Word, we may embrace,
and ever hold fast the blessed hope of everlasting life,
which thou hast given us in our Saviour Jesus Christ.

CRANMER. Sir, I have a book to offer the King:
a sacrament of the Word; deign, sir, to behold.

ONE OF THE COMMONS. In the wall of the creed
the stones of doctrine hold,
built there, at need,
by prophets and doctors of old:
maxims of James and Paul
and John, master of all;
out of the Sacred Books
the True Faith looks.

ANOTHER OF THE COMMONS. Great are the logical schools
but greater are myths and songs:
Solomon's lions and bulls,
Jael and Israel's wrongs;
the books are filled with shapes and sounds,
and heaven opening thunderous bounds
where feet-and-face-hidden seraphs burn
and eyed wheels turn.

ANOTHER OF THE COMMONS. Maxim and myth are shaped to
bones;
mine grow older and truer to these.
Where Absalom dies and King David moans
my head with Job is bowed to my knees,
Dry is the green, brittle the tree
where the Lord sits to throw taunts at me;

this book is man's breath
'twixt the first and second death.

        [CRANMER *brings the Bible to the* KING.

CRANMER. Many identities hath the Sacred Word,
   so widely is he bestirred for our beatitude:
   always, in each good, somewhere he hath his height
   that the flight of man's heart must find. O but speech
   never found reach of wing or vision more
   than soars here! since the Catholic faith began
   man here has had his shelter, light, and food.
   It were good, might it only be so, for men
   with this alone to live, Nazianzen said,
   and do no song other. Apollyon's thong
   hath bound this now for these hundred years
   from native ears and native sound. O now
   our common English, whereto we were born, left
   forlorn of this health, yet having and meant to have
   wealth so great of words, language of power,
   this hour receives its consummate miracle; the Word
   takes the sound heard natively around,
   the excelling grace of speech; in our proper land
   deigns He—O marvel!—to stand; this is His type,
   ripe for communion, this His image. Sir,
   let the King's grace bountifully prefer
   this; enfranchise Christ into English speech.
THE KING. Is not your coat of arms badged with three
   cranes?

CRANMER. Sir?

THE KING. Three cranes, I say?

CRANMER.   Sir, yes.

THE KING.   They shall be pelicans,
   pelicans in their love, feeding their thankless young
   on their own blood. I have changed them; see it done.
   You are like to be tested, if you stand to your tackling:
   but have your will, publish it under my seal.

THE SKELETON. Under my seal, too, whereby I promised it
   to you.

1545   My hour is not yet come, but I will show
   a little prelude of the hour of you and me.

> [*He goes and stands behind the* LORDS.

THE FIRST LORD. Who stands by the King?

THE SECOND LORD.   The King's friend.

THE FIRST LORD. A silly innocence lives in his face.

THE SECOND LORD. It hath caught the King—unlike to
   unlike.

THE FIRST LORD. Is he apt to be used?

THE SECOND LORD.   Apt to be used,
   being shy of his own heart and mind,
   but not so apt—none of his kind are—
   if you trouble his incalculable sense of honesty,
   which holds the King; who now has none,
   only a kind of clinging to honesty in others.

THE FIRST LORD. He prayed the Court to renounce the holy
   days

forbidden to the Commons; he has a dæmon
of peace and the poor.

THE SECOND LORD.   They are quite dangerous,
these hankerers after peace and goodwill;
they are provoked by I know not what
to be a stone everyone stumbles on—
except the King.

THE FIRST LORD [*after a pause*]. Except the King.

THE PRIEST [*coming up to them*]. Lords, Master Cranmer hath
the King's ear,
urging heresies, hurrying destructions,
preaching impossible simplicities of doctrine.

THE FIRST LORD. He thinks Christ as simple as he is.

THE PRIEST. Save, Lords, the ancient miracle.

THE FIRST LORD. We are altogether against miracles,
new or old.

THE SECOND LORD. But the old are better,
since men forget how miraculous they are,
and the King gives more land to their protectors.
Come, let us put an end to this fellow.

THE FIRST LORD. He has had none of the abbey lands.

[*They go up to the* KING.

Sir, please your Highness permit

THE SECOND LORD. an examination of Dr. Cranmer.

THE FIRST LORD. He has infected the realm with heresy

THE SECOND LORD. desperately provoking perilous commotions,

THE FIRST LORD. dangerous to your Majesty,

THE SECOND LORD. dangerous to your Majesty.

BOTH LORDS [*speaking in the* KING'S *ears*]. Commotions,
    uproars, rebellions, conspiracies!
  hear the Commons!

THE COMMONS [*murmuring*]. Grievances, grievances!
  Where are the abbeys?

                    the rites?

                              the mystery?

  Give us back the things our fathers had!
  Strange men are sitting on top of the abbeys,
  stamping on our rites, stealing our rents.
  Come to the King: grievances, grievances!

THE LORDS. Sir, you were best commit him to the Tower;
  it is clear your Commons do not care for communion;
  that, we think, is the meaning of their noises.

> [*They come between the* KING *and* CRANMER, *back to
> back, with outspread arms. The* FIRST LORD *advances,
> driving* CRANMER *back before him; the* SECOND *stands
> over the Throne.*]

THE SKELETON. If these men had their way now,
  they would save him difficult life, difficult death;
  and me the working, but I must divide
  his life to the last crack and pull his soul
  —if it lives—through the cracks; therefore—

> [*He whispers in the* KING'S *ear.*

THE KING [*roaring*]. Thomas!

THOMAS CRANMER OF CANTERBURY

Where is Canterbury?
where is the Archbishop?
Keep him waiting, do you, among your boys,
in the scurvy noise of your lackeys, your runabouts,
    hey?
I say, by my faith I have a fine council; this man
that is better than the proudest of you, the King's more
than any in his true heart, what, you would start
as a cony, would you, and dog-chase on to his doom
with fellows that will find room to spare and to swear
this or that slander for a crown or two? I will put you
    down,
masters: come hither, Archbishop; this is the man
I owe much, by my faith in Almighty God.
I will nod you to your death before him; I vow
there shall none of you touch the man the King loves.

[*The* LORDS *retire.*

They are gone; I have saved you awhile; but yet
this life, lord Archbishop, is a catcher of men,
aye . . . aye . . . it shall catch you.

[*The* SKELETON *comes up and sits at the* KING'S *feet.*

CRANMER. Sir, I desire no more.

THE KING. Y'are an honest man. Listen: I had a dream.
    I saw a creature run about the world,
    everywhere at all times, that would be caught
    but would not stay for catching, or mayhap
    the thing was still, it was everything else ran by,

and I ran also, too slowly or too fast;
sometimes I could see, sometime I could not see,
but when I saw I wept for the joy of it—
a crimson flashing creature, full of power.
All my life I sought for it, and then I died,
and it was gone and everything was gone,
except a voice calling, *Where is the prey,*
King of England? but I was not the King: it called
Henry, where is the prey? but I was not Henry.
In the nothingness, for the creature was not, I stood
and answered: *I*—and before I added more
the nothingness broke over me in a peal
of laughter, all the angels crying *You!*—
Here is a fellow calls himself I,—and their mirth
filled me, but I was weeping; there were streams
of mockery running to misery; and I woke,
the tears upon my cheeks, and the chamberlains trembled
beside me, hearing me roaring in my sleep.
What did I say that was wrong—am I not I?
am I not I myself? what did this mean?
CRANMER. Sir, I do not know.
THE SKELETON.   You will know.
                    [*To the audience*] So will you.
THE KING. I have always lost the thing I sought to find,
   you are the nearest thing I ever found
   to the thing that I looked for; you are an honest man,
   God shall be honest with you and play you fair;
   God help you in the hour when he plays you fair.

Yet I am the King, and Henry, and myself.

I always lose the thing I seek to find.

Catherine was forbidden, and Anne was false, and the Howard.

Why have so many been false to me—to *me?*

Yet one man pleaded—who? for Anne, for the monks, for Mary, for the traitor Fisher, the traitor More, and the worse traitor Cromwell. Who, I say?

CRANMER. Sir, I believed they loved you.

THE KING.   Nor they nor me.

You are the nearest thing to a friend I have.

I have saved you, Archbishop; come up to me; what is this?

THE SKELETON [*touching the* KING]. Give the King thy judgment, O Lord!

THE KING. Thomas, I am dying: hold me, speak to me.

CRANMER. Highness!

THE KING. I have saved you; I have loved you.

CRANMER.   Sir, my lord,

think upon Christ!

THE KING. I have loved you, if not them.

You are the only thing that was true to me.

I have loved you.

CRANMER.   King Henry, think on Christ alone.

THE KING. I shall be I, shall I not?

CRANMER.   Sir, if God please.

THE KING. Love me, Thomas; hold my hand; look to the heir.

                                        [*The* KING *sits rigid.*

C

THE SINGERS. In all time of our tribulation, in all time of
our wealth, in the hour of death, and in the day of judgment:

ALL THE PERSONS [*kneeling, except the* SKELETON *and the*
KING]. Good Lord, deliver us.

> [*The* SKELETON *removes the crown and leads the*
> KING *out,* CRANMER *following. The* LORDS *whisper in*
> *a corner. The* SKELETON *returns and crouches at the*
> *top of the steps.*]

THE SKELETON. Ohé, the King is dead.
Protection is taken away; the world grows unkind.
The man must carry himself; his mind
follows its vision after its mode
through the uneasy palace to its god's abode;
Ohé, the King is dead.
The twin hungers are loosed; an amphibian shape
monstrously crawls from dungeons of need;
from bedchambers of greed a chattering ape
stands hatted by the man's side.
Yet bounty and beauty and others' thoughts abide
still at his back for belief.
He finds not awhile the place of derelict grief,
the mean little oubliette,
where he and I, cheek by jowl, shall be comradely met.
Ohé, the King is dead.
Now there is no sure face in the man's mind;
fingers are fumbling at his wrists, trying to bind;

feet tripping his feet, to throw him down;
the lords and the commons come crying about the town.

THE COMMONS [*moving towards the throne*]. King Henry is EDWARD
    dead. VI
              1547–53

       King Edward is on the throne.
Long live the King!

            God save King Edward the Sixth!
He is a pretty boy!

         and pious.

               Where is he?

God bless him!

       bring him out!

            show him!

                where is he?

Show us the King!

THE LORDS [*putting on their hats and standing by the Throne*].
    Be silent.

THE COMMONS.   The King! show us the King!

THE LORDS.   Be silent.

      [*They perch on the arms of the Throne.*

We have the King in our guard; the King is a child,
though a paragon of precocity, much too precious
to march through a hubbub of hurras; his state of health
renders it rash to let him shine in public.

         [*They lift up the Crown.*

Be still, and know that we are the Lords.

THE COMMONS.   The King!

THE LORDS. The King is behind us and in us; we are the
    King:
we shall rule England for thrice a hundred years.

    [*The* COMMONS *maintain a continual subdued murmur.*
    CRANMER *returns, habited in a gown.*]

CRANMER [*going up to the* LORDS]. My lords, King Henry had
    in mind to make
a ritual for communion, that men should find,
by nourishment on the supernatural, the natural
moving all ways into the supernatural,
and the things that are below as those above.
Do not forget this work; our honour, Lords,
is to order the land according to God and the King,
if King Edward permits.

THE FIRST LORD.   We are the King's protectors.
Go to it, Archbishop.

THE SECOND LORD.   Go to it, Archbishop.
We are making a ritual for our own communion
on lands, houses, chantries, abbeys, guilds,
which are broken for us, and blood is given for us.
Feeding on that body, we grow; we grow into houses
lustily foundationed over leagues of land.
Our bodies are made space and our blood time.
Enlarged so, a man's spirit has nothing,
nothing at all between himself and God.
Sacraments of nature are better than those of grace,
and a simple noble heart than copes and mitres.

But do not you trouble for that; go you
and use your patterns of words, versicles, responses,
formulæ, vain repetitions, muttering and mummeries.
We will deal with you at need as you deal with words;
the King permits you to write your soul in words.

CRANMER. My lords, the purified Church is the truer Church,
Catholic and Apostolic; a simple heart
may err without the means.

THE SECOND LORD.   We will not err.
One King is dead; the gentry do not die.
One King is a child; the gentry are never children.
Whatever bruises their heel, they bruise its head,
and now the older miracle seems the more troublesome.

THE COMMONS [*crying out*]. Down with new-fangled com-
munions! down with the rich!

[*Some of them run down the steps and face the stage.*

ALL. Grievances! grievances! hear the Commons' grievances!

VOICES. Give us back something we can pray to!

Give us back the thing that hangs in the Church.

Give us back our shows and songs!

We will not have the Mass said in English!

We desire Latin and processions and a great to-do!

We will not have the Bible printed in English!

We will not have two sorts of communion.

We will not have communion more than once a year.

We will have a mystery, a wonderful thing.

Everybody shall bow and touch their foreheads,
and any one who does not shall immediately be slain.

Grievances! grievances!

ALL. Hear the Commons!

> [CRANMER *speaks from the top of the steps.*

CRANMER. You ignorant rough creatures, you rocks and
    heaths,
who will have the mystery of Christ to be no more
than an unintelligible monster, risen
from your and your fathers' past, the lapse and beat
of time through something hung in a shell of gold,
you ask you know not what: because of my office
and my duty to God and the King, now will I say
what you should know and cannot: therefore hear.

THE SKELETON [*while* CRANMER *continues to address the
    rebels*]. How absolute we are! now in your night
is there no ravage? does nothing, Thomas, roar
like seas or winds or the crowds of the poor marching?
is all hushed down to those sweet-sounding collects
where reason and charity softly kiss each other?
You were less certain in old days at Cambridge.
This is the ruinous nonsense of the mind,
that men come mightily to believe their causes,
because of their mere rage of controversy,
and without morality to believe in morality.

CRANMER. Alas, it was never anywhere heard till now

that this sweet and comfortable food
Christian folk should curmudgeonly deny!
and yet be willingly stupefied with substitution—
ceremonies, genuflexions, adorations.
Has not our Lord the King made you a path?
To rest in images is clear superstition;
refuse them; come from them; come into gentle peace.
THE SKELETON. You speak well, Thomas, but you do not
    know all.
No man ever refused adoration yet,
but in it was something which was death to refuse;
death of one kind or another, I say not which kind.
CRANMER [*stumbling in his speech*]. And this . . . and you
    think . . . and you, children,
want a thick mystery to gaze at. Mystery
is there to be resolved by the soul's mathematic.
There are two classes of men—godly and ungodly;
those who desire experience of the only good,
those who refuse it. Children, will you refuse?

[*The* LORDS, *with drawn swords, fetch him back.*

THE FIRST LORD. Leave them to my Hungarians, Archbishop.
THE SECOND LORD. I have collected a great unity of
    Christendom—
Germans and Italians, Lutherans and Catholics,
mercenaries from abroad of every faith,
gospellers and idolaters; all 's one.
They shall teach the English to defy the Families.

THE FIRST LORD. Seymours, Dudleys, Pagets and Howards.
  Down, dogs!
THE SECOND LORD. To your mire, swine!
CRANMER. My lords, the poor—
THE FIRST LORD. Leave the poor to us, Archbishop;
  we will see to the security of Crown and Gospel.
THE SECOND LORD. We are the things below as the things
    above;
  the source, not to say father, of word and spirit,
  the word of our culture and the spirit of our gospel.

> [*They run down, threatening the* COMMONS.

THE SKELETON. Beautiful on the hills are the feet of the
    heralds
  of the kingdom, bloody as Christ's but with others'
    blood.
  Since the Adam in Eden invoked and dividing yoked
  themselves separately to the bitter angel of possession,
  since the secession and embroilment of the sons of
    Noah,
  to certain chosen spermatozoa is revealed,
  semper, ubique, the propriety of proprietorship,
  the rite and religion of themselves;
  see how they fight for their Vincentian canon,
  which, among those who believe it for a season,
  is called natural Decency and obvious Reason.
THE SINGERS. Thy word is a lantern unto my feet: and a
  light unto my paths.

THOMAS CRANMER OF CANTERBURY

I have sworn, and am steadfastly purposed: to keep thy
righteous judgments.

I am troubled above measure: quicken me, O Lord,
according unto thy word.

Let the freewill offerings of my mouth please thee, O
Lord: and teach me thy judgments.

[The LORDS *drive the rebels out and follow them.*

A WOMAN [*running out from the other* COMMONS *and kneeling*
   to CRANMER]. Hear of the thing, Sir, you have made
   dear!
Sir, how it clings and sings, this Bible, this book,
lifting one look to scry heaven, speeding the sound
underground of power; joys
and griefs, mingling in its noise, spring from our Lord
who works deep down; there is Christ adored,
and his Spirit lurks, more than ourselves, in our mind
behind moons and suns: no day
but expands, as it may, from this. My mother died
with whispers of it; I make a guide
for my son's mind of portions I hear read.
Let it spread, Archbishop, let it rise,
this is a good way for a man to be wise.
CRANMER. It shall blow as the wind of youth; it shall take
   youth
with wonder, nor age lose it nor death deny.
The Word to wayfaring men shall testify
how his graces transubstantiate times and places,

THE
BOOK OF
COMMON
PRAYER
1549-52

nor shall any release from the claws of John's eagle
this land, till the poor find peace, and the rich goodwill,
and the course be one with its end.
Faith herein shall befriend for ever our folk,
hope, and the thing that is more than hope or faith.
Thus it saith for ever: O gift, O grafted power
in the power of men's souls: Christ singer, Christ voice,
    Christ song,
in hamlets, towns, ages: rejoice, rejoice,
heart! feed on this! what remains?
O but this—that words be as muscles and veins
to Christ's Spirit bringing communion, the shape
of his advent, nor none there to escape
into the unformed shadow of mystery mere,
but find a strong order, a diagram clear,
a ladder runged and tongued; now my hand,
my unworthy hand, shall set itself to that end.
Be for the need of the land the ritual penned.

> *[He goes to his desk.*

THE SKELETON. Rungs and tongues! the anatomy! the ladder
    and the scale!
Your hand shall be a banner, friend, in another manner,
when another fire burns than this sweet desire.

> *[To the audience.*

And you, whose hands are still, lying now so quiet,
one day, against your will, I may bid them move
in their own life; then they shall crawl

slowly up sides, shoulders, and heads,
till each spreads
palms and fingers there, and waggles assent
to all sins I call against them. Thomas, you may think,
was fortunate in his hand beyond you. But that can wait.

CRANMER [*writing*]. Almighty God, unto whom all hearts
be open, all desires known, and from whom no secrets are
hid; Cleanse the thoughts of our hearts by the inspiration
of thy Holy Spirit, that we may perfectly love thee, and
worthily magnify thy Holy Name;

THE SINGERS. Through Christ our Lord. Amen.

THE SKELETON. Take heed, my people, take heed to your
praying.
You shall give account of your least saying:
who knows how far your words may go?
It were good you said but *yes* or *no*.

CRANMER [*writing*]. Lift up your hearts:

THE SINGERS. We lift them up unto the Lord.

CRANMER [*writing*]. Let us give thanks unto our Lord God:

THE SINGERS. It is meet and right so to do.

CRANMER [*writing*]. It is very meet, right, and our bounden
duty, that we should at all times and in all places, give
thanks. . . .

THE SKELETON. Ah how the sweet words ring their beauty:
it is meet, right, and our bounden duty.
but will you sing it with unchanged faces
when God shall change the times and the places?

CRANMER [*writing*]. . . . here we offer and present unto thee,

O Lord, ourselves, our souls and bodies, to be a reasonable, holy, and lively sacrifice unto thee; humbly beseeching thee, that all we, who are partakers of this holy Communion, may be fulfilled with thy grace and heavenly benediction. And although we be unworthy, through our manifold sins, to offer unto thee any sacrifice, yet we beseech thee to accept this our bounden duty and service; not weighing our merits, but pardoning our offences, through Jesus Christ our Lord; by whom and with whom, in the unity of the Holy Ghost,

THE SINGERS. all honour and glory be unto Thee, O Father Almighty, world without end. Amen.

THE SKELETON. Many a master hath made device,
in words, of incomparable sacrifice,
but woe, woe,
to any who see not where the words go:
it were better they had said but *yes* or *no.*

CRANMER [*writing*]. We praise thee, we bless thee, we worship thee, we glorify thee. . . .

THE SKELETON [*leaping up*]. We praise thee,

THE SINGERS [*joining with the* SKELETON]. we bless thee, we worship thee, we glorify thee, we give thanks to thee for thy great glory, O Lord God, heavenly King, God the Father Almighty.

CRANMER [*writing*]. The peace of God which passeth all understanding. . . .

THE SINGERS. keep your hearts and minds in the knowledge and love of God.

CRANMER. These to the will of God in the will of the King.
　Who waits?
THE SKELETON. I. After such a prologue,
　whatever faces you see, or hear feet go by,
　they are only I, points and joints in me;
　I only waiting for what I only am working.
CRANMER. Who waits?
THE SKELETON [*going to him*]. My lord!
CRANMER. 　　　　　　　　　Friend, do I know you?
　Are you of my household?
THE SKELETON. 　　　　　An indweller, my lord;
　a copier-out, a carrier-about
　of works and words, an errand-runner.
CRANMER. My eyes are weak; forgive me, if I should know
　you.
　Much study, it is written, tires the flesh.
THE SKELETON. Much study of such communion tires the
　flesh,
　though perhaps less than the communion itself tries;
　your eyes, my lord, need certain sovereign balsams
　of spittle worked in clay and cleansed by fire
　I may one day bring; it will help not a little.
CRANMER. What are you called?
THE SKELETON. 　　　　　　Anything, everything;
　fellow, friend, cheat, traitor.
　I was born under Virgo, of an outlandish house,
　to keep account of such vows as there are written.
　My name, after to-day's fashion, is latinized

into Figura Rerum. Anne prized me at first;
later she found my bones and called me a cheat.
King Henry found me a servant, and then a traitor.
I am the delator of all things to their truth.

CRANMER. My mind and eyes are blind; what are you?

THE SKELETON.   To truth;
to what you say you would find: I believe you; find it.

CRANMER. I am blind; I am afraid; what are you?

THE SKELETON. A moment's geometrical formation of fate;
a functioning spectrum of analysed eternity;
eternity always insists on being analysed.
I will call you, for you bade me show you the end,
no more servant now, but friend.
Do you run to me or do I run to you?

CRANMER. God, without whom nothing is strong—

THE SKELETON. I respected you, Thomas; I heard; I am here.
Do not fear; I am the nothing you meant.
I am sent to gather you into that nothing.
Do you run to me or do I run to you?

CRANMER. Christ or devil, leave me to lie in peace.

THE SKELETON. If I leave you to peace I shall leave you to
lie,
to change without changing, to live without living.
I will not. Do you run to me or do I—

CRANMER. God, God, stop the world moving!

THE SKELETON. Stop me loving, would you? stop me
proving
the perfect end in the diagram of bones?

You believe in God; believe also in me;
I am the Judas who betrays men to God.
Friend, friend!

CRANMER.   Ah, ah, ah!

[*As he falls forward, his hands clutch his papers;
he seizes them and straightens himself.*]

My work! I have a work.
I am nothing except—

THE SKELETON.   I must run then after you.
You will choose the rack instead of the cross?
I am sorry, friend; it takes longer.
I will remember your prayers and meet you
in the core of the brain, in the coasts of the heart,
drawing apart, doubling and troubling you.
Of all my Father gave me I will lose none.

CRANMER. The Council: I must go to the Council.
The King is dead; the book goes to the Council.
Almighty God, unto whom all hearts be open—

[*He hurries out.*

THE SKELETON [*calling after him*]. Yours is; a little while,
and we meet at Oxford,
and she who is to come, the queen who sends you there,
I will have her too; I will catch her as well as you.

[*He turns suddenly on the* COMMONS *who are moving.
They rush out in confusion.*]

And all you—I will lose none.
In your lives and tongues I will bring you to climb

at my time, without haste, without sloth,
the rungs of my ladder, where the redeemed
walk; his lordship dreamed
it was set from his English hand in the English land,
but the anatomy itself talks, talks of itself.

> [*The* COMMONS *have gone out; he continues to the
> audience.*]

How I speed, how heedfully I speed!
Can you wait? can you see me coming? can you wait?
for a little while and where am I? lo,
a little while and here am I; spin,
spin each of you his brave platter,
his work, his life! how it topples and falls!
No matter; spin, platter! spin, world; spin,
air and prayer, without and within, but one
twirling twy-flash dazzle of soul and sun
down the hangman's way on the hangman's day;
can you pray now or be shut-eye dumb?
can you pray: *Even so, Amen, Lord, come?*
as my singers—O hark! as my singers say.

> [*He backs out, beckoning to the* SINGERS, *who rise and
> follow him.*]

THE SINGERS. Here we offer and present unto thee, O Lord,
ourselves, our souls and bodies, to be a reasonable,
holy and lively sacrifice. . . .

PART TWO

The SINGERS *enter and take their places.*

THE SINGERS. My God, my God, look upon me, why hast
thou forsaken me: and art so far from my health, and
from the words of my complaint?

O my God, I cry in the daytime, but thou hearest not:
and in the night season also I take no rest.

And thou continuest holy: O thou worship of Israel.

[CRANMER *enters.*

CRANMER. Lambeth and Westminster are full of strange
song.
A voice but now cracked from the street like a thong
high to the sky, stinging all ears with *Wait,*
wait, singing *the day of the hangman's way.*
I sit in my study; a fit of fear takes my heart
while in my mouth the grand art
fails, speech fails; the thong cracks to the sky;
at the song the souls out of each part of heaven fly;
heaven is thick with spirits flying and crying,
fleeting towards me, and fleeing off ere we meet:
Tyndale was burned; Forrest was cruelly burned—
behind them the souls of the righteous ride in the air;
God be witness I never turned in my mind
or denied, but always sought and desired to spare;
the souls come rushing, flushing, with crimson light,

D

and the words in my book slither out of my sight
as if they were that creature the King's look
caught, new creatures my thought cannot find
while my mind shrinks from an unknown singer in the
    street.
Hark now, hark!

ONE OF THE COMMONS [*coming in secretly*]. Archbishop,
    Archbishop,
now when the shaft is shaped from the quill
to aim at the brain, to whistle shrill
against us who are slain for need and not for will,
who saved others and ourselves we cannot save—
Christ pardon us talking on the edge of the grave—

Archbishop, Archbishop,
against us who all our lives on our tongues have rolled
for sweetness of taste God's terms, now we take hold
on a saint unhallowed, a martyr unaureoled;
saying, *so Christ made us, Christ be merciful so,*
Christ pardon us, speaking more than we know.

                         [*He goes to his place.*

CRANMER. The world is full of a threat that forms not yet.
O peace, peace! all we are strangers
each to his brother, each for another
ingeniously inventing temptations and cruel dangers.
Once and twice I have written Melanchthon to come;
he who ingeminated peace to Germany,
he who is nearest in kind of all men to me;

he writes not, he comes not. And we,
we ever reform our books and not ourselves,
but the storm in the street is whipping our books from
   their shelves,
stripping torn pages, driving white-breasted prayers,
to swoop and stoop and trouble the day,
blinding and stunning us running on a sloping way.
Melanchthon my brother, come from Germany, come:
let us make a council of peace for Christendom.
Is it he? is it he? not he, but now for our sin
time's anguish and anger and bitter clangour begin.

> [*The* COMMONS *enter noisily; the* PREACHER *runs in,
> dragging the* PRIEST.]

THE PREACHER. My lord, my lord, here is a knave
   whose parish is weary of him; his bells ring
   in the time of sermon; sometimes he sings
   in the choir ere sermon is done—nay,
   even challenges godly preachers in the pulpit.
   The whole parish is a witness to it all.
CRANMER. This were ill done indeed; is it truly so?
THE PREACHER. My lord, he was once an abbot on Tower
      Hill;
   shows his breeding.
THE PRIEST.   I do not say, my lord,
   but sometimes, ere sermon is ended, a bell will ring,
   or I cry *hem* and turn in my seat, or even
   think the preacher were done and begin to sing

before the good man had unburdened all his stuff.
Old habits die hard, my lord, and accidents happen
in churches as well as out.

CRANMER. What is your church?

THE PRIEST. I am Vicar of Stepney, if it please your Grace.

THE PREACHER. But the people of Stepney are weary of him,
my lord.

CRANMER. It is very ill; we must be tender to consciences
when we suffer by them; we must in charity
believe that a good man labours at his duty,
though it should please God plague us by his duty.
Get hence to Stepney, vicar, and hear the sermons.

THE PRIEST. At your Grace's bidding.

[*He retires.*

THE PREACHER. My lord, ye are over-gentle
to so stout a papist!

CRANMER. Why, we have no law to punish them.

THE PREACHER. Were I Archbishop, I would fast unvicar
him;
and put sharp sentence on such rogues as he.
If it come to their turn, they will show us none
of this foolish favour.

CRANMER. Well, if God provide it so,
we shall abide it.

THE PREACHER. God shall snatch the sword
from those who will not use it on his foes.
Y'are warned.

CRANMER. Be off, good fellow; do we serve Christ
   by running round with torches, bludgeons, and oaths?
   Who was it the torchbearers once found in the garden?
   the bludgeon-brandishers brought into court?
   the oath-takers smote and smothered?
   I am troubled often because, in my jurisdiction,
   I have signed and sent obstinate men to the fire.
   Amend your life; love all; make your communion
   on love and peace—this is the body of the Lord.
THE PREACHER [*retiring*]. Now I see why the great people
   laughing say:
Do my lord of Canterbury a shrewd turn,
and he is your friend for ever. But God—
God has only us to defend his glory,
and what will happen to that if we leave off killing?
       [*He goes over to the* LORDS *who have entered, the*
       SKELETON *following.*]
THE SKELETON [*coming down*]. My hour is nearer; I will
   show myself again.
The way he treads is turning into a rope
under my hands; he pauses; I pick it by a trick
from under his feet, and fling it to these hands that fling
   it to those,
each time circling his body: he feels the pain
constrict his rich arteries—love, and faith, and hope:
tight round his drawn muscles the pressure grows.
Did he gird himself to tread my way? he is girt
now by the way, and borne therein to his hurt

by my multitudinous hands. I am his match
to delay and dismay. Catch, my children, catch!

[*He makes a motion of throwing a rope to the* LORDS,
who, with the PREACHER, *come near* CRANMER.]

1552 THE SECOND LORD. In this order for the supper of the Lord,
what is this, Archbishop, about kneeling
to a memory, to a past day, to creatures and men?

THE PREACHER. In the Word of God there is no word of
kneeling.

CRANMER. Nor standing nor sitting; lie then on the ground—
bivouac as Turks or Tartars, around salvation.

THE SKELETON. Or—might it be said—after the mode of the
Apostles?
Controversialists are apt to forget the facts
till a certain jangle of my bones comes to remind them.

THE SECOND LORD. No kneeling; the grace lies in the
memory.

CRANMER. I grant it is not given by measurement,
weight, or solidity; it is immaterial;
how can the flesh absorb spirituality?

THE SKELETON. Ah, you do not quite know, incredulous
Thomas,
what the flesh can do when it is put to it.
You shall do a thing one day with the flesh of that hand
to astonish men as God may astonish you.
Is not the world full of his witness?
what of the light that lighteth every man?

THOMAS CRANMER OF CANTERBURY

[*Running to the edge of the stage and calling to the* COMMONS.]

Have you forgotten, have you forgotten,
how you saw and handled aboriginal glory,
sown from spirit, seeding in flesh?
what is the plot of each man's story
but the wonder and the seeking and the after-sinning,
O bright fish caught in the bright light's mesh?

[*The* COMMONS *stir. He swings round.*

O master and doctor, have you forgotten
when the woman Joan came out of the tavern,
and her face was moulded of heavenly fire?
or how you looked from your Cambridge cavern
and saw King Henry God's spoken splendour?
Shall I, the splendour and the glory, tire?

[CRANMER *staggers. The* SKELETON *runs and leaps
on the Throne.*]

Have you forgotten, have you forgotten,
O my people, have you forgotten,
The moment of central and certain vision,
when time is faithful and terrors befriend,
when the glory is doubled by the sweet derision,
in the grace and peace of the perfect end?

Have you forgotten, have you forgotten,
O my people, have you forgotten,
the moment when flesh and spirit are one,
—are they ever separate, but by a mode?

Though the skull look out, will you fear, will you run?
will you forget how the glory showed?

> [*He pauses and leaps down.*

But I intermit the metaphysical dispute
between my lord of Canterbury and his peers.
There is this to be said for my lord of Canterbury,
he dimly believes in something outside himself—
[*He adds generally to the Audience*]
Which is more, I can tell you, than most of you do.

> [*As soon as the* SKELETON *descends, the* SECOND
> LORD *sits down on the Throne.*]

THE SECOND LORD. Y'are slack, y'are slack, Archbishop:
   why do you loiter?
CRANMER. It is rumoured, my Lord, you have shut up in the
   Tower
   one of the Bishops; that the revenue of the See
   must be accommodated to your Grace.
THE SECOND LORD. We will say to the King: it is put so in
   the papers.
CRANMER. I must tell you this is against all honesty.
   It were good you stayed till the King came of age.
   I must tell you we serve the King; where is the King?
THE SECOND LORD. I am King enough; you shall not see the
   King,
   unless by me. I have a plan for the Throne.

1553   [*He plays with the Crown.*

The judges agree; the Council agrees; all men

50

agree to the plan I have made. The King agrees.
The King commands you to agree.

CRANMER.   I will see the King.
It is my right: I will see the King alone.

THE SECOND LORD. You shall not see the King more than I
   let you,
nor alone, nor with any of your loyal, simple sort.
The King commands you, on your allegiance, agree.

CRANMER. If the King commands—

THE SKELETON.   The rope begins to constrict.
Something happens Doctor Cranmer had not foreseen
when the King commands something against the king-
   ship.
There may be worse coming. Hark!

ONE OF THE COMMONS [*running out*]. The King is dead.

> [*A trumpet sounds at the entry. The* COMMONS *rush* QUEEN
> *on to the stage. The* PRIEST *runs forward. The* MARY
> 1553-8
> SECOND LORD *rises.*]

THE COMMONS. God save Queen Mary!

THE SECOND LORD [*to the first*]. Shall we stand together?

THE FIRST LORD. I doubt we cannot stand.

CRANMER. Is King Edward dead? I must wait then for the
   Queen.

> [*A second trumpet. The* COMMONS *shout.*

THE SECOND LORD. Can she alter the world?

THE FIRST LORD.   That we shall see presently.

CRANMER. I would I were not so afraid.

THE SKELETON.   The rope constricts.
Hope is beginning to feel a little choked:
Faith soon. Love—we shall see presently.

[*A third trumpet. The* QUEEN *advances. A* BISHOP
accompanies her.]

THE SKELETON [*leaping up and down the steps*]. Fly, Thomas.
CRANMER. Bid our friends fly, not me.

[*The* PREACHER *runs out.*

THE SKELETON. Your Bishops fly.
CRANMER.   Well; but I cannot fly.
I will not turn from the things that I have done.
THE COMMONS. God save the Queen.
THE SKELETON. She is coming on you; you will lose your
    See.
CRANMER. It was given by God and the Prince, and it is theirs.
THE COMMONS. God save the Queen.

[*The* LORDS *take off their hats.*

THE COMMONS AND THE LORDS. God save the Queen.
THE SKELETON. She is coming; you will lose your honours.
CRANMER.   Have I any?
Neither honours nor dignities—nor money hardly:
I was richer when I came to Lambeth first.
But money and life belong to God and the Prince.
THE SKELETON. She is coming; you will lose your honour.
CRANMER.   If God please;
    they roared my courage out of me when I was young.
Yet, if God please, I will stand to what I have done.

THE SKELETON. Your mind and your world make nonsense
of your life.

She is here; my hour is at hand; now I am yours.

> [*He goes to the back.*

ALL. God save Queen Mary.

> [*All the* PERSONS *kneel, while the* QUEEN *takes her
> throne, the* BISHOP *beside her.* CRANMER *rises. The*
> QUEEN *kneels. The* SKELETON *exhibits himself in the
> attitude of one crucified.*]

THE SINGERS.

> Tantum ergo sacramentum
> Veneremur cernui:
> Et antiquum documentum
> Novo cedat ritui;
> Præstet fides supplementum
> Sensuum defectui.

> [*The* SKELETON *comes down the stage; all the* PERSONS
> *crouch lower as he passes. He faces* CRANMER *at the
> opposite corner.*]

THE SKELETON. The writings yield to the Rite; the Rite
to me.

This is the end, friend, of all translation,

when your bones are translated to what you loved and
hated.

> [*The* QUEEN *rises and sits.*]

CRANMER. When King Henry told me his dream I dared not
speak

of the beak of the King's falcon, but well I knew
how it flew through my sleep, as now; a slither of wings
beats on my face and brings
a hot iron to my heart; in the dream I cannot shriek
nor speak; my heart stops; I am nailed,
impaled by that motionless heart to the air or what there
where I hang the air is. I float; each limb
at its own whim begins to jerk and gyrate
or at some power's ruling the hour; they dance,
I live askance in a jest, the puppet of the prince
of the air, long since damned, I damned long since.
Christ help me! my heart dead,
my body spread, my mind lusting to walk,
handle, learnedly talk: but each jerk
of the limbs lurks in the brain, becoming babble
of words, words unmeaning, insignificant gabble,
words infinitely dividing; infinitely sliding
smoothly, faster and faster, before and behind each other:
mind and body, nothing stops or drops or ends till I wake.
God have mercy upon me for Christ his sake!
First when I came to Cambridge, wretched man;
in the night ere Anne died, again when the lords
accused, or of late were fain destroy: but this last
darkness was wholly passed so, dream into dream
cast, sweat into sweat, fear into fear;
when the Queen from the depth came rising, riding so
    near:
when the Queen came riding yesterday into the town;

she had no head, over her shoulders the Crown
threw a golden light; her hands emerged on the rein;
at her horse's pacing my limbs jerked in pain,
as the Queen rising, riding, came steadily in.
Purge, O God, a sinful man of his sin.

[*He bows himself.*

THE SKELETON [*standing over him*]. When the heart has no
   motion, the brain no thought,
we shall see what we shall see;
he shall find into what plight he was brought
when we bade his desire be.
He had his way; if he trod his way,
where there's a way there's a will;
many there be that find the way,
few that find the will.

THE SINGERS. Lighten our darkness, we beseech thee, O
   Lord, and by thy great mercy defend us from all perils and
   dangers of this night.

[*All the persons rise.*

ONE OF THE COMMONS. Master Cranmer has made sub-
   mission.

ANOTHER. He has made adoration.

ANOTHER. He has set up the mass again at Canterbury.

ANOTHER. It is false; he gave the Bishop of Rochester a
   paper.

THE PRIEST. God has put down the mighty from their seats.

THE FIRST LORD. It is fortunate then that he chose to put
   down the Archbishop

whom the Queen's grace can heartily condemn for heresy;
The question of sedition may be quietly dropped.

THE SECOND LORD. After all, the Dudleys were never really
gentlemen,
Lady Jane was making difficulties already.

CRANMER [*standing up*]. I raise again the mass at Canterbury?
It was a false and flattering monk who did so.
Have I erred? let them show me then where I have erred.

THE SKELETON. In thinking, though it was important for you
to be right,
it mattered at all in the end whether you were right.

CRANMER. I stand by all the doctrine of the Church.
The Scripture and the Fathers are agreed—
it was given for communion and not adoration,
and it was made idolatry everywhere.

THE   THE QUEEN. Thomas Cranmer, falsely called Archbishop....
DEGRADA- CRANMER [*going to her*]. Madam,
TION
1555–6   your father made me. . . .

THE QUEEN.   who unmade my mother,
discrowned her and disthroned the Holy Thing. . . .

THE SKELETON. O tares! O wheat; that grow together to
harvest:
I run with you, O my people, through the dark air.
Thomas, your heart that was double with God and the Devil
must be choked by a heart double with the Devil and God.

THE QUEEN. . . . will you recant now?

CRANMER.   What should I recant?
Madam, your Grace, by God's grace, is the head

of all the people of England, therefore the head
of the church they are: one folk, one Church, one head.

THE BISHOP. The Queen has denounced you to the Holy
Father.

CRANMER. Ah, that the Queen should denounce her subject 1555
to a stranger!

THE FIRST LORD. Madam, this treachery shocks me.

THE SECOND LORD.   We have come, Madam,
to entreat your Grace to restore adoration and the Pope
who has been of late a stranger only by accident,
by a slight misunderstanding about motherhood.

THE FIRST LORD. We have drawn up an act for the restoration,

THE SECOND LORD. adding
a second part to prevent interference with property.
If the abbey lands were ours when we were Protestant
they will clearly be closely ours when we are Catholic—
not that we are ever anything in fact but ourselves.
We are the proprietors; we are time and space.

THE FIRST LORD. With that corollary, behold us wholly
yours.

THE SECOND LORD. And dispose of the Archbishop in any
way you choose.
Every contract involves a little sacrifice.

THE SKELETON. When time and space withdraw, there is
nothing left
but yourself and I: lose yourself, there is only I.

THE BISHOP. The Holy Father, by his sentence, here
deputes us to degrade you. Thus—and thus.

1556 CRANMER. Which of you hath a pall to take my pall?

THE SKELETON. I. [*He wrenches the crozier from* CRANMER'S *hand, and gives it to the* BISHOP. CRANMER *is unfrocked and a coarse gown is put on him.*]

THE SINGERS. O Lord God of my salvation, I have cried day and night before thee: O let my prayer enter into thy presence, incline thine ear unto my calling.

For my soul is full of trouble: and my life draweth nigh unto hell.

Thou hast laid me in the lowest pit: in a place of darkness, and in the deep.

My sight faileth for very trouble: Lord, I have called daily upon thee, I have stretched out my hands unto thee.

I am in misery, and like unto him that is at the point to die: even from my youth up thy terrors have I suffered with a troubled mind.

Thy wrathful displeasure goeth over me: and the fear of thee hath undone me.

They came round about me daily like water: and compassed me together on every side.

My lovers and friends hast thou put away from me: and hid mine acquaintance out of my sight.

THE BISHOP. Now you are no lord any longer, nor priest; you are excommunicate.

CRANMER.   I appeal from all to the Council of the Universal Church.

THE BISHOP. But the Universal Church has cast you out.

THE SKELETON. Thomas, what is happening now is more like

the counsel of the Universal Church,
the operation of the body of Christ,
than any language.
Things spoken seem unfamiliar when they happen.

[*He stands opposite* CRANMER *at the top of the steps,
in the attitude of a priest in procession.*]

THE QUEEN. Will you recant?

CRANMER. I will always submit myself
to the Church, and the Pope if the Pope be head of the
Church,
if they can prove me that out of the Scriptures.

THE SKELETON [*taking a step*]. That just unfrocked you; will
you be unfleshed?

THE QUEEN. It shall not serve; will you submit yourself
to adoration and our Father at Rome?

THE BISHOP. Hilary, Augustine, Ambrose, Chrysostom,
Tertullian—
will you set yourself up against these?

THE QUEEN. We are the Prince, as our father was the Prince:
will you set yourself up against us?

THE BISHOP. If the Pope is head of the Church, obey; if the
Prince
and the Prince admit the Pope, why, still obey.
Will you set yourself up against your principles?

THE SKELETON [*taking a step*]. There is an hour—this,
Thomas, is the hour—
when the pure intellectual jurisdiction

THE
RECANTA-
TIONS
1556

E

commits direct suicide: the mind and the world
die, and the life shivers between their bones.

CRANMER. If the Queen serve the Pope, I will serve the
Queen.

THE QUEEN. This shall not serve; we have signed the writ
for the burning.

THE BISHOP. But see, what quiet might come instead of
burning!

THE SKELETON [*taking a step*]. And no man can think clearly
while he is burning!

Though, we agree, that is neither here nor there.

What is incineration compared to truth?

THE QUEEN. Consider the command of the Prince who is as
a god.

THE BISHOP. Consider the witness of doctors to the will of
God.

THE SKELETON [*taking a step*]. Consider anything with a re-
mote resemblance to God

that is likely in the least degree to save you from burning.

[*A pause.*

CRANMER. General Councils have erred and Popes have
erred:

is it not like that my word went wrong?

THE SKELETON. It is like.

CRANMER. That when I strove at winning the land for Christ
I erred from the beginning?

THE SKELETON. From the beginning.

CRANMER. Christ my God, I am utterly lost and damned.
I sin whatever I do.

THE SKELETON.   Whatever you do.

CRANMER. As well sin this way and live as that way and die.
It is folly and misery all.

THE SKELETON.   Folly and misery.

CRANMER. Did I sin in my mother's womb that I was forsaken
all my life? where is my God?

THE SKELETON.   Where is your God?

                                            [*After a pause*

When you have lost him at last you shall come into God.

        [*The papers of recantation are brought to* CRANMER.

CRANMER [*signing them*]. I will sign anything, everything.
I have burned,
and the flame is returned on my soul: if it saves from hell
I may well recant; they may be right; they are,
for they say they are, they are sure, they are strong. O
Christ
—Christ leaves me to myself, I lose myself,
as I lose him; I will believe adoration,
I will receive the Catholic Church of the Pope,
I will put my hope in images and substitution;
I sinned in the false dissolution of King Henry's matter.
Bring me all; I will acknowledge all.
I was the master of a whole college of heresies—
faster! faster!—I am the worst

that ever the earth bore, most outcast, most accurst
... Korah ... Saul ... the penitent thief ... O Christ,
what have I done?

THE SKELETON. What have you done?

THE BISHOP.   These
unforced, with a pure consent, you freely deliver?

CRANMER. I have signed, I will sign, all; freely I will sign.

THE SKELETON. There are two freedoms, brother; this is one.
Between now and to-morrow's sun you shall come to the
other.

THE BISHOP [*returning to the* QUEEN]. Madam, the apostasy
is ended; Cranmer recants.

THE QUEEN. To-morrow then, let him be given to the fire,
and let the recantation be publicly proclaimed.

ONE OF THE COMMONS. Master Cranmer hath recanted.

THE PREACHER [*creeping in*].   No; he dare not!

ANOTHER OF THE COMMONS. He has sworn the Pope back
again into England.

ANOTHER. No; that was done but now in the Parliament.

ANOTHER. They will not burn him then?

ANOTHER.   Yes, he will burn.

THE PREACHER. He has betrayed—

THE PRIEST.   He is restored to—

BOTH.   truth!

THE SINGERS.

THE
MARTYR-
DOM

20 March
1556

Dies irae, dies illa,
Solvet saeclum in favilla,
Teste David cum Sibylla.

CRANMER. They will burn me; I know it; I denied God for
  naught.
THE SKELETON. Some men deny, some men declare; unless I,
  who shall try the denial and the declaration?
  I will try it in my way, not yours nor any man's else.
CRANMER. They will burn me.
THE SKELETON.   What is that, O soul, to
  thee and me?
  Thomas, all your life you have sought Christ
  in images, through deflections; how else can man see?
  Plastic, you sought integrity, and timid, courage.
  Most men, being dishonest, seek dishonesty;
  you, among few, honesty, such as you knew,
  in corners of sin, round curves of deception;
  honesty, the point where only the blessed live,
  where only saints settle, the point of conformity.
  Mine is the diagram; I twirl it to a point,
  the point of conformity, of Christ. You shall see Christ,
  see his back first—I am his back.
CRANMER. Can life itself be redemption? all grace but grace?
  all this terror the agonizing glory of grace?
  but what will they do? will they pardon or burn?
THE SKELETON. I am Christ's back; I without face or breath,
  life in death, death in life,
  each a strife with, each a socket for, each,
  in the twisted rear of good will, backward-running speech,
  the derision that issues from doctrines of grace
  through the division man makes between him and his place.

Christ laughs his foes to scorn, his angels he charges
with folly; ah, happy who feel how the scorn enlarges!
I am the thing that lives in the midst of the bones,
that (seems it) thrives upon moans, the thing with no face
that spins through the brain on the edge of a spectral voice.
Rejoice, son of man, rejoice:
this is the body of Christ which is given for you;
feed on it in your heart by faith with thanksgiving.

CRANMER. Will they burn me?

21 March   THE SKELETON.   Friend, do you hear the
1556   horses, the horses?

Do you hear the gentlemen riding to town?
Lord Williams of Thame and Sir Robert Bridges,
and Sir John Brown and his Oxford neighbours,
the gentlemen riding into town?

[He begins to sing.

for the burning of a poor man, a very poor man:
a poor man in duty, God save him from duty!
a poor man in honour, God save him from honour!
a poor man in misery, God save him from misery!
All Christian people, pray for a poor man!

[He runs to the edge of the stage and sings outward.

All Christian people, God save you from riches!
if you have duty, God save you from duty!
if you have honour, God save you from honour!
if you have misery, God save you from misery!
God make you poor men for the burning of a poor man.

THE SINGERS. He hath filled the hungry with good things,
and the rich he hath sent empty away.

[*Two* EXECUTIONERS *enter, carrying torches. They
stand in the middle of the stage. The* SKELETON
turns, still at the edge of the stage, and looks at
CRANMER.]

THE BISHOP [*coming to* CRANMER]. Master Cranmer, have
you any money?

CRANMER.   No.

THE BISHOP. Here are fifteen crowns to give to the poor.

THE SKELETON [*singing*]. At the bringing out of a poor man,
a very poor man.

CRANMER. Why does he talk of crowns?

THE SKELETON [*running to him*].   Friend,
traitors and heretics, common criminals, lazars,
are given alms for the poor. Lazar, set forth.
Mayhap someone will give you such alms on your way
as shall make you rich for ever with another's riches.

CRANMER. They will burn me then?

THE SKELETON.   Friend, it is necessary,
they will tell you; love necessity; I am he,
I am coming, run—run hastily to meet me.
You shall find that in me is no more necessity. Run.

CRANMER. I will run, I will run . . . [*He stops, choking.*]

THE SKELETON.   I will run faster than you.
I will run faster than this man's words or yours.
I am the only thing that outruns necessity,

I am necessary Love where necessity is not.

> [*They fetch* CRANMER *to the centre of the stage. The*
> BISHOP *goes as to a pulpit, the* SKELETON *following*
> *him and standing behind him. A noise from the*
> *crowd.*]

THE BISHOP. Behold him, good people!

THE SKELETON [*copying the* BISHOP'S *gesture*]. Behold him,
  covenant of Christ!

THE BISHOP. Though he repent, it is needful that he burn
  to make equilibrium with the Lord Cardinal John
  who died for defending as this man for destroying.

THE SKELETON. I have made equilibrium; I have drawn him
  level.

THE BISHOP. And for other just causes known to the Queen
  and Council
  which now must not be opened to the common folk.

THE SKELETON. For the cause of the justice that I will
  thoroughly open
  on the day when I do so well that ye cannot think.

THE BISHOP. He that stole from England the food of the soul
  weeps, repents, is saved as the thief that rose
  from a cross by Christ to the promise of Christ's own
  cross.

THE SKELETON. The Son of Man comes as a thief in the night.
  After my mode I have gathered many souls;
  who shall prevent me, coming swiftly for all?

> [*The* QUEEN *rises.*

THE BISHOP. This child of Apollyon is saved; infinite grace!

THE SKELETON. Infinite, without measurement or dimension,
the contradiction of measurement and dimension;
I only measure what I only am.

THE BISHOP. Lest any man doubt his repentance, his conversion
he shall tell you ere he die; Master Cranmer, speak.

THE SKELETON. I am equated now to his very soul:
I am his equilibrium; Thomas, speak.

CRANMER [*kneeling*]. Blessed Omnipotence, in whom is heaven,
heaven and earth are alike offended at me!
I can reach from heaven no succour, nor earth to me.
What shall I then? despair? thou art not despair.
Into thee now do I run, into thy love,
That which is all the cause thou wert man for us,
and we are nothing but that for which thou wert man,
these horrible sins the cause of thy being man,
these sins to thy love the cause of motion in love,
where is stayed no sin nor is merit of ours marked,
nor aught can live but the hallowings of thy Name,
through which thy kingdom comes, in earth and heaven
thy will being done, the bread of which be our food.

THE SKELETON. And I lead you all from temptation and deliver from evil!

THE SINGERS.   Amen.

CRANMER [*rising*]. Good people, give not your minds to this
glozing world,

nor murmur against the glory of the Queen;
love each other, altogether love each other;
each to each be full of straight goodwill,
wherethrough let the rich give naturally to the poor
always, and especially in this present time
when the poor are so many and food so dear.
What else? yet for myself I will something say:
I am quite come to believe in Omnipotent God
and in every article of the Catholic Faith.
But since the Queen will have me cut from obedience,
outcast from her, I must have an outcast's mind,
a mind that is my own and not the Queen's,
poorly my own, not richly her society's.
Therefore I draw to the thing that troubles me
more than all else I ever did—the writings .
I let abroad against my heart's belief
to keep my life . . . if that might be . . . that I signed
with this hand, after I was degraded: this hand,
which wrote the contrary of God's will in me,
since it offended most, shall suffer first;
it shall burn ere I burn, now I go to the fire,
and the writings, all writings wherein I denied God's will,
or made God's will but the method of my life,
I altogether reject them.

> [*A pause. The* SKELETON *goes to the top of the steps.*
> *Then an uproar.*]

FIRST LORD. Are you in your wits?

SECOND LORD.   Do not dissemble.

CRANMER.   My lords,
    I am a man loved plainness all my life,
    nor ever till lately dissembled against the truth,
    which now I am most sorry for.

THE BISHOP.   Stop his mouth.

VOICES. Away with him to the fire!

> [*The* EXECUTIONERS *run out.*

                                        He is mad with rage!
    He despairs, he despairs!
                            The devil hath his soul!
    Blessed be God for the good man's word!
                                                    Blessed!
    He does not know what he says!

THE SKELETON.   But I know all.
    Friend, let us say one thing more before the world—
    I for you, you for me: let us say all:
    if the Pope had bid you live, you would have served him.

CRANMER. If the Pope had bid me live, I should have served
    him.

THE SKELETON. Speed!

CRANMER.   Speed!

ALL THE PERSONS.   Speed!

> [*They all hurry out.*

THE SINGERS. Glory be to the Father, and to the Son; and
    . to the Holy Ghost; As it was in the beginning, is now,
    and ever shall be: world without end. Amen.

Milton Keynes UK
Ingram Content Group UK Ltd.
UKHW031201241024
450188UK00004B/329

9 781528 708494